Fairies of Kawakawa

Fairies of Kawakawa

Tiffany Wagstaff

Fairies of Kawakawa published by Rangitawa Publishing, Feilding, New Zealand. 2019.

©Tiffany Wagstaff
All rights reserved

No part of this publication may be reproduced in any form or by any means without the prior permission of the author and publisher.

ISBN 978-0-9951166-0-3

www.rangitawapublishing.com
rangitawa@ xtra.co.nz

For Alice

E iti noa ana nā te aroha
A small thing given with love

Acknowledgements

Amber, thank you for your unfailing excitement.

PART ONE

1

Once upon a time, on a little farm not far from here, lived a girl named Alice. She lived with her mother and father, and her scruffy little black dog named Molly. There were goats and chickens in front of her house and a little orchard behind it, and all around there was a forest named Kawakawa.

Kawakawa wasn't very big; a fantail could fly it with one swoop and a swift wind. But the trees were twisted and knotted with vines, and the ground was steep and covered with moss. Like all lovely things, the little forest was surprisingly wild. The air was cool, the light was green, and everything was peaceful. As a wee babe, Alice would wander through Kawakawa with her mother and father, on paths that had somehow appeared by themselves. And as she grew, so did her love for the forest. She would hunt for hedgehogs and flowers and treasure. She delighted in birdsong and in turn the birds sang for her; it was their way of saying "thank you" for Alice's gentleness with their home.

Rabbits lived there, and frogs that were greener than spring grass. There were birds and bugs and butterflies that flew around Alice's head when she visited. And something else lived there, too.

Fairies!

One day, when the air was still and damp and the sun shone mottled on the forest floor, Alice and her father were in Kawakawa collecting fallen wood. Alice wandered away from her father; she was drawn to a patch of the "melting mushrooms" that often appeared throughout the forest.

But Alice discovered something that she did not expect, something she had not seen in all her time spent in the forest. There, tucked behind the melting mushrooms, at the bottom of a tall tree, was a tiny door.

Alice gasped – a door! Imagine that! She was afraid to blink in case the little door disappeared. Alice turned and saw her father at the other end of the clearing, lifting heavy branches into the wheelbarrow. When she turned back it was still there, the little wooden door that looked old and worn but was very, very new to Alice. It had a little iron handle and two tiny hinges, with a brass door knocker shaped like a tear drop. In front of the door was a step made of tiny grey pebbles.

Well, Alice was no stranger to surprises in Kawakawa. She knew about the magic in the forest before she even knew what magic was, but the older she got the more she saw the enchantment around her. So, taking a deep breath, she decided to see just how magical this little door was.

"Hello?" Alice whispered. "Is there anybody home?"

The door creaked open. There was someone home indeed…

From behind the door peered a tiny person. She had bright green eyes and skin that looked like it was sparkling. She peeped to the left of the door, and then to the right, and then, for just a moment, she looked at Alice. But as quick as a flash, the door shut and the little person was gone!

Alice gasped.

"Come back!" she whispered urgently, not wanting her father to hear.

"Go away!" Alice heard clearly in an equally urgent whisper. The little person sounded very rattled.

"Please come out," Alice begged, "I promise I won't hurt you."

"No one is home!"

Alice paused. "But – but I saw you."

"You imagined it!"

Alice was annoyed. She certainly did not imagine any such thing!

"But you're talking to me! And I can see the door!"

After a few moments, Alice heard the latch click and the door opened a crack.

"You can?" asked the little person.

"Of course, you're right there. Please, come out."

The door swung open and there, right in front of Alice, was a fairy. An unmistakeable, undeniable, honest-to-goodness fairy. Wings and all! She had a shimmering purple-blue dress, white hair that wisped around her head like loose spider's webs, and a pair of bright purple wings. The fairy had quite forgotten Alice was there, and was standing on her doorstep with her back to Alice, hands on hips, looking at her own door. She huffed, kicked it with her tiny bare foot, and then stomped back inside, slamming the door behind her.

Alice sat back on her bottom and crossed her legs. She watched the door intently, and for a long while nothing happened. Her father had taken a load of wood to the house and come back again. The sun moved in the sky. Birds sang. And eventually, Alice heard the tiny person's voice again, loud and clear.

"Even though there is nothing here to see, are you still out there looking?"

Alice felt excitement bubble inside her.

"Yes," she whispered. "Please, come and talk to me. Who are you?"

The door opened and there appeared the fairy again, eyeing Alice suspiciously. Alice grinned. She couldn't believe her luck! The fairy sighed and, bending in to a low, dramatic courtesy, spoke to Alice in a more courteous, friendly manner.

"Alice, I am Beryn, a Kawakawa fairy and owner of this useless broken door that has forgotten to be invisible." The door, at that moment, shut by itself and pushed the fairy a little forward. She told it to shush.

"And you, young Alice, are the first person in all our lifetime to have waited long enough to see."

"See what?"

"See us, silly girl."

Alice heard something move behind her. She turned and saw her father at the edge of the clearing. He went on working as dozens of tiny people emerged from the trees and bushes all around her. Alice was

16

surrounded by fairies, fairies that were smiling at her and not at all afraid.

And why would they be? These fairies had known Alice her whole life. They had watched her talk to tiny animals that were sick, they'd watched her dance with bubbles and thistle seeds, and they'd listened to her sing. They felt her happiness when she found toadstools and her fear when the nasty dog from next door ran through Kawakawa. They were Alice's oldest and dearest friends.

2

Alice's father picked up the handles of the laden wheelbarrow and turned to face Alice. The fairies Alice had just met didn't even flinch – except one little fairy with yellow wings who batted her long, glittering eyelashes at him! Alice tried not to pull a face.

"Allie, I'm taking this wood up. Are you coming?" The fairies turned to look at Alice, waiting for her answer. Could he not see all these shimmering faces in the trees?

"Um, no, I'm staying here. I'm talking to some friends..." Alice had said this many times but in this moment she wasn't kidding. Her father just shrugged, told her not to touch the mushrooms, and heaved the wheelbarrow out of the clearing. As he disappeared in to the forest, a few of the fairies waved goodbye.

"My dad can't see you…" Alice said slowly. Beryn shook her head.

"Nope! Daddy is sweet but far too busy to know about us. The trees love him, though. So does Neiolith." Alice saw the little yellow fairy sigh so deeply she fell head first in to a clump of cape daisies, sending puffs of pollen in to the air. Alice giggled. Beryn rolled her eyes.

"You call him 'Daddy'?"

"Well, yes. That's his name."

"Paul is his real name," Alice asserted, but Beryn waved this fact away like a bad smell.

"We don't bother ourselves with what is real – we only care about what is lovely."

Alice furrowed her brow, wondering what Beryn meant. She decided to change the subject.

"So how many of you are there?"

"Well, there's more than two, that's

for sure. There's one, and two..." Beryn pointed to various fairies but was starting to look a little confused. In the end she shook her glistening wings and said with an air of confidence, "There are many ones of us, Alice, and we all know you. We know you, and we know you know, and we know you know we knew about you, before you even knew you knew."

Alice frowned. Beryn huffed in exasperation.

"You've been talking to us and about us and for us since the moment you stepped into our forest, even though you couldn't see us." Beryn did a quick curtsy, and some of the other fairies followed. "Wee Alice, we are forever grateful."

Alice grinned. Her own fairy friends! Not being able to contain her happiness, Alice leapt to her feet and did a little twirl in the clearing. Jumping on the spot she exclaimed breathlessly, "I knew it! I knew there was something about this forest! Too many things happened here for no good reason!" She stopped jumping when she heard the fairies gasp. "Other than magic," Alice corrected herself, "And that is a wonderful reason!"

She threw her hands out into the air. Alice danced again in a circle, her joy so strong that it drew the fairies from their hideaways in the bushes. They joined in her dancing, fluttering around her like a glittering whirlwind as soft as feathers.

And then, breathless, Alice stopped. She realised something that made her heart drop.

"I suppose I'm not allowed to tell anyone about you all." She looked around her at the dozens of little faces. "If I tell people about you, will you disappear? Do I have to keep you a secret?"

Beryn fluttered over to Alice and hovered in front of her face.

"Wee Alice, you couldn't keep us a secret if you tried with all your might. Don't you see? You've told everyone you love about us! Goodness, Mummy could speak hedgehog with all you've told her about the forest!" Alice opened her mouth to ask about *speaking hedgehog*, but Beryn rattled on.

"We are no secret. We are hard to find and very rare, but like all things rare we need a little bit of protection. And you can't protect something if you don't know about it, right?"

"I suppose you're right…"

"Of course I'm right. No, Alice, don't keep us secret. In fact, tell the whole world about us!"

Alice grinned. Talking was one of the things she was really very good at.

22

"That sounds wonderful," she exclaimed. She looked around her again and said, "I simply cannot wait to get to know every single one of you."

Just then, Alice heard her mother's voice in the distance. "Alice! Haere mai ki tō kai!"

"But right now I have to go!" Alice ran down the path to head out of the clearing but stopped short. She turned around, and saw all those beautiful little fairies. They were real, they were lovely.

"I'll come back tomorrow. You'll be here?"

"We always are, wee Alice."

3

"Mum, do you believe in fairies?"

"What's not to believe?"

"You always say that…"

"Must mean it's right, then."

Alice was sitting at the table with her mother while she worked on the laptop. Her father was out stacking wood, having already finished dinner. Alice was still having hers. Oh, how she loved chewing.

But her mind was elsewhere tonight. She just couldn't get those fairies out of her head. And now that she was inside, having the same old conversation about make-believe with her mother, Alice was starting to doubt herself. She had imagined all sorts of wonderful things in Kawakawa before. What if this was just one of those times when she had lost the line between real and dreaming? And her mother was no help –

an opinion one way or another was harder to find than a frog in winter.

"Mum, I saw fairies today."

"You did?" Alice's mother glanced sideways.

"Yep. One is called Neiolith, and she loves Daddy."

"She does?" Alice's mother looked away from the screen at Alice. "Neiolith is a beautiful name for a fairy," she said.

"I don't know why she loves him." Alice's mother smiled, and Alice went on. "But the trees love him because he's nice to the forest."

"How do you know that?" Alice's mother asked.

"Beryn told me."

"Is Beryn another fairy?"

Alice nodded and her mother smiled wider.

"It sounds like you had a very exciting

time in Kawakawa today, my baby."

"I did, Mum. There were so many fairies. And they've known me since I was a baby. Did you know that, Mum? Have you ever seen them?"

"I can't say I have, I'm afraid," said Alice's mother, shaking her head. Alice looked down at her plate, her heart sinking. Her mother saw lots of things – if she hadn't seen the fairies, maybe she did just dream them up.

"But that doesn't mean they aren't there," her mother went on. "You saw them today, didn't you?" Alice nodded and looked up.

"I don't know why, but fairies don't show themselves to adults often. I think we forget how to see stuff like that when we get older. But I wish I could see them, and if you keep talking to them you might never forget how to do it."

Alice thought for a second, chewing.

"Mum, can I go to the forest again tomorrow?"

"Of course, little muffin. I want to hear all about your new friends."

4

Alice still had a mouthful of toast and jam as she skipped down the driveway to the edge of Kawakawa. She simply couldn't wait to see the fairies again. It had been a sleepless night; Alice had lots questions for the fairies, and she had so much to tell them herself. Despite her excitement, she stopped halfway down to greet the goats.

"Morena, Audrey! Kia ora, Rupert!" Rupert ignored her as always, but Audrey bleated an equally chipper morning greeting, then frolicked down the fence line alongside Alice. Alice liked Audrey; she was always happy when you were, even if she didn't always understand why. Alice tickled her white velvet nose before running down the hill to the gate that led in to Kawakawa.

Alice arrived at the clearing, a little

puffed from running and anticipation. And there, at the base of the big tree, was the door. She breathed a sigh of relief – it hadn't been a dream! Alice felt the air tremble against her cheek, then suddenly Beryn was sitting on her shoulder, stretching her arms above her head.

"Good morning, wee Alice," Beryn yawned drowsily. "Did you have a restful sleep?"

"Not at all, Beryn," Alice replied, trying to talk very quietly for fear her voice might knock little Beryn off her shoulder. "I was far too excited to sleep!"

With Beryn on her shoulder, Alice walked carefully towards the side of the clearing where a fallen log served as a seat. Alice was suddenly very aware of how big she was, with this very small person sitting so lightly next to her head. She wondered, for a worrying second or two, if she'd ever accidentally stood on one of them. Alice sat down. Beryn fluttered off her shoulder and took a seat on the log, too.

"So, what are we going to do today?" Beryn asked.

"I want to know all there is to know about fairies!" Alice announced. Beryn's jaw dropped.

"Everything?! But there is so much! I wouldn't even know where to begin!"

Alice giggled. "Well, maybe not everything, but I want to know as much as you can tell me! What are the names of all your friends? Do you have magic powers? Is it just fairies that live here or are there other magical creatures, too? Are there any boy fairies? Why can't Mum and Daddy see you? What is your dress made out of? What would happen if —"

"Alice." Beryn held her hands up in front of her, stopping the flow of Alice's wonderings.

"Yes?"

Beryn took a long, slow breath. "My dear. We have sooo much time to talk about such things, and it's sooo early in the morning!" Beryn threw her hand over her eyes and fell backwards, lying on the log next to Alice. But Alice was itching to learn all she could about her new friends!

"Please, Beryn!" Alice pleaded. "Please tell me about the fairies!"

Beryn peeked out from under her arm and screwed her tiny nose up. She sighed, and made a big performance of hauling her little body upright. She sat down on the log next to Alice.

"Oh, all right then. I'll answer one question now but then we are going gecko hunting."

"Deal!" Alice agreed enthusiastically. She sat, waiting for Beryn to talk, her whole body wriggling. But Beryn was just sitting there, staring at her. Eventually Beryn raised her arms to the sky.

"Well, what's the question?" Beryn said, a little smile tickling the edges of her lips.

"Oh!" Alice thought for a moment. There were so many. Where did she want to start? Finally she asked, "Beryn, how did you come to live at Kawakawa?"

Beryn fluttered her little wings, lifting herself in to the air. "Now that is a very good question, wee Alice," Beryn mused as she settled herself on Alice's knee. "That question takes me back some time. Hmm..." She seemed deep in thought, so Alice waited patiently.

She thought how wonderfully normal it felt, to have a fairy sitting on her knee in the middle of her forest. She wondered if she'd see any of the others today, and if they'd join her for the gecko hunt, one of her favourite games. She felt the warm morning sun on her face as it shone down through the clearing. Beryn cleared her throat, letting Alice know she was ready to begin. Alice focused all her attention on the little fairy, still sitting comfortably on her knee.

"For a long time, I didn't have a home. I couldn't find a place that sang the same as me, the hum was never right. So I went on an adventure, to find where I belonged…"

5

BERYN'S STORY

For a long time, I didn't have a home. I couldn't find a place that sang the same as me, the hum was never right. So I went on an adventure, to find where I belonged. I used to live a long way away, in a place where the trees grew straight and separate. It was colder there, but not unpleasant, and I loved the snow. And my family were happy there, too. They flew about in the meadows and enchanted the castles that the humans were building. But the hum of the land made me feel uneasy and restless.

Fairies can feel the earth breath, can hear it sing, can feel it vibrate with life. A fairy can live one hundred lifetimes in one thousand places and call each one her home, but her magic is strongest when the hum of the earth matches her own. She sings in harmony with the songs that the land has being singing since the beginning of time.

34

And so, when I came of age on my one hundred and second birthday, I set off across the water. My family stood on the edge of the cliff as I flew over the sea. I was scared to leave them, but the further I flew away from the hum that didn't feel right, the stronger and braver I could feel myself becoming.

I flew for days before I reached a small island. I was tired. The messages of love that my family sent through the vibrations of the earth kept me going; but I needed to rest, and this little island looked perfect. There was nothing there, other than a few trees. There were no humans and certainly no fairies. I found a coconut and, after filling myself up on the sweet water inside, I climbed in. Before long, I had fallen in to a deep, deep sleep.

I was in such a deep sleep that I didn't even hear the storm. The coconut I was inside was swept off the beach and tossed out to sea. I woke up while the storm was raging around me, thrashing and crashing against the walls of my coconut! I was too scared to look outside. I had been in storms before but not on my own in the middle of the ocean! Luckily, the coconut was holding strong against the fierce weather, so I sat with my back against the soft, white wall inside, wrapped my wings around me like a blanket, and thought sunny thoughts.

It felt like forever but eventually, the storm calmed. I peeked through the hole in the coconut to find myself floating in clear blue water, quite calm, with a still, grey sky overhead. And in the distance was land, green and wild looking, with a veil of clouds hovering over top. Even though I was so far away I could feel it, humming so sweetly it brought tears to my eyes. I dipped my fingers in to the cold blue sea and felt the hum in the water. I knew, at that moment, sitting in a floating coconut, that I had found home.

Back then, forests like this little one covered most of the land. There were no roads, no power lines, just the forest and some people. Back then, the hum was much louder and everything that lived here knew how to sing with it. I did too, I soon found out, and before long I had made friends with all the birds that lived here. I loved the forest – there were tall, straight trees like where I came from, but others looked like they were reaching out to each other with sideways trunks, twisted vines, and flax fronds that grew long like fingers.

And, oh my, the fairies! Some had travelled to this land like me; they were also drawn by the hum of the land. Some, Ngā Patupaiarehe, had lived here for as long as the earth had been breathing, and sang with the hum so perfectly it made you want to weep. I quickly found myself a part of a family, a family of travellers who had found our home on the doorstep of Ngā Patupaiarehe.

6

Alice sat on her log seat, wide-eyed and open-mouthed. There were even *more* fairies? Beryn, though, let out a happy sigh and flitted into the air.

"Gecko-hunting time!" Beryn exclaimed. But Alice wanted to know more.

"But Beryn," Alice began, "tell me more about Ngā Patupaiarehe! Are they here? Will they sing for me if I ask them?" Alice looked around her. There were perhaps a dozen fairies that she could see now; they had woken and emerged during Beryn's story and were not paying a lot of attention to her. The fairies were all dressed in clothes that looked to be made from dyed spider's web. Some were chatting, some were collecting things off the ground, and one older-looking fairy was sweeping the small step in front of her door. But there were no fairies that seemed interested in singing for her.

Beryn shook her little head. "Oh no, wee Alice, Ngā Patupaiarehe like to keep themselves to themselves. They live up there, in the twisted trees on the hill." Beryn pointed toward the steep bank on the other side of the driveway, covered with writhing vines and old, knotted trees. "They live under the trees, in houses made from vines, not inside the trees like us. We call that hill The Burrows."

"The Burrows? Daddy hasn't talked about any houses under the trees. Surely he could see them?"

Beryn raised an eyebrow. "But how often does Daddy really go up there?"

Alice thought hard. She couldn't remember ever seeing her father on that hill. In the end Alice looked at her feet.

"I suppose he doesn't. But he could if

he wanted to…"

"Of course he could," Beryn agreed. "But he doesn't, and that is why Ngā Patupaiarehe have settled there. Because although humans are close, they don't stray into their forest. They are safe there."

Alice was indignant. "They don't have to worry about me! I wouldn't hurt them, or their forest."

Beryn shrugged, unconvinced. Or maybe she was just bored by all this talk of Ngā Patupaiarehe?

"C'mon, Alice, you promised one story then we'd find a gecko! Are you coming?"

Alice gazed up toward The Burrows one more time, before following Beryn to the little stream where the geckos often hid.

It only took a minute to arrive at the stream, a trickle of rainwater that ran down from the bank – The Burrows – through the trees and down to the dam. There were flat, smooth rocks and damp, dead leaves all over the ground; a perfect home for the tiny lizards. When Alice and Beryn arrived at the lowest part of Kawakawa, Alice noticed a fairy already sitting there on a rock, inexplicably holding a long fishing rod over the water.

As they drew closer, Alice's eyes widened. This fairy was a man! An old man with a long white beard! And a set of glorious red wings that glistened in the soft morning breeze! He was sitting very still, gazing up in to the tree in front of him. Alice followed his gaze and found he was watching a fantail dance around the leaves. Very slowly, the old man fairy lowered his fishing pole and scraped around in the damp leaves just in front of him. A few seconds later the fantail darted down and joined in the scratch. The man's smile grew so wide his cheeks pushed his eyes closed. Soon the fantail found a tasty morsel and gobbled it down, making the old man chuckle silently.

Beryn quietly made her way over to the man and sat next to him. She kissed his cheek in greeting and he gave her hand a squeeze. Beryn pointed to Alice, still standing a few metres away behind a tree, and beckoned her to come closer. The movement made the fantail stop digging around and fly back to the safety of the high branches, but the old man's smile didn't fade.

"Uncle Mort, this is Alice. Alice, Uncle Mort," Beryn announced. Alice gave a little smile and Uncle Mort flew up to meet her. He may have looked older than old, but he moved just as quickly and gracefully as Beryn. He hovered in front of Alice and smiled at her – a warm, friendly grin.

"Wee Alice, it's so wonderful to finally talk to you properly. Come, sit. Feed Olivia with me," he said, gesturing towards the fantail in the tree. "What have you young scamps been doing?"

Alice sat on the ground next to Beryn and said, "Beryn told me about how she came to live here, in the forest, and now we're looking for geckos…" Alice looked at Beryn to see if there was anything to add.

"Alice wants to meet Ngā Patupaiarehe."

Uncle Mort chuckled. "Do you now, dear?"

Alice nodded. "They don't need to be afraid of me. I'd love to meet them."

"They just like to keep to themselves, dear. They're happy up there by themselves."

"Do you visit them?"

He thought about this question

carefully. "Sometimes," Uncle Mort nodded eventually.

"Can you tell me about them?" Alice asked, hopeful. But at that moment, Beryn heaved a loud, dramatic sigh.

"I'm going looking for geckos! Have fun, Alice. Once Uncle Mort gets started, he doesn't stop!" Alice thought this was quite cheeky but Uncle Mort just smiled. Alice picked up a stick and used it to shuffle some leaves. Olivia, in the tree, watched with interest.

"I want to know everything, Uncle Mort, and I have all day."

Uncle Mort looked back up at the tree where Olivia sat. He whistled to her and then waited for her response. He and Alice sat quietly for quite some time and Alice wondered if he hadn't heard her. Just as she was going to speak, Uncle Mort cleared his throat.

44

* * *

Alice heard her mother call. It was lunch time. She had spent all morning sitting next to Uncle Mort, listening to his whispery, gravelly voice telling her about Ngā Patupaiarehe. Beryn had long gone, but other fairies had collected water from the stream, and had come to sit with Uncle Mort and his peace for a while. Some had brought food to share with them both.

And now it was time for Alice to go. She thanked him, really and truly, and made her way back out of Kawakawa. On her way back to the house she looked back at The Burrows, trying to imagine another group of fairies up there, looking down on her, feeling frightened of her. She promised herself that she make friends with Ngā Patupaiarehe, too.

7

Once again, Alice ran past the goats with a mouth full of food. She was just too excited to eat her lunch at the kitchen table, and her mother was exasperated with trying to make her sit still. In the end she pressed the sandwich in to Alice's hand, put the apple and biscuit into Alice's school lunch bag, and told her to eat in the forest. Alice was three steps out the front door before she realised she'd forgotten the bag!

But Alice didn't go straight to the forest's clearing. Instead she walked the edge of Kawakawa, following the driveway to a tree stump on the sweeping bend. There she sat, with the forest behind her, eating her sandwich and gazing up to The Burrows. It really was wild up there; the hill was almost vertical and covered in trees that grew so close together it was impossible to tell where one stopped and the next began. It really was the perfect place for fairies who were scared of humans to live. It would be very tricky to get into those trees and even harder to do anything in there, like work or play.

But years ago, when Alice was just a baby herself, a storm had caused some of the hill to slip away. Her father left it to grow back on its own so it was not as wily and wild as the rest of The Burrows, and the ground wasn't as steep. Alice chewed thoughtfully.

"Lelice!"

Alice jumped and turned quickly around to see Neiolith flitting towards her. These fairies sure had loud voices for creatures so small. In no time the little fairy was beside her, her yellow wings and dress shimmering like a droplet of sunshine.

"Kia ora, Neiolith, how are you?"

"Oh, Lelice, I'm so sad!" For a moment, Neiolith's beautiful little face dropped in to a pout. Alice asked her what the matter was, and only wondered for a half-second why Neiolith called her *Lelice*.

"All the old fairies are meeting to talk about what jobs need doing, since Spring is nearly over, and I'm not allowed to go! I'm nearly ninety years old, practically an adult! And just because I help flowers bloom doesn't mean I can't be helpful after Spring! 'Go and play,' they say. 'Go and have fun, Neiolith!' they say. Oh, wait, what am I complaining about? Oh, Lelice, isn't this forest just gorgeous? And I'm free to enjoy it! Lelice, why are you frowing?"

Alice was frowning because she was trying with all her might to follow Neiolith's breathless avalanche of words, which had changed direction and come to a halt so suddenly!

"Oh, um, I'm fine. Neiolith, what do you mean you help the flowers bloom? What jobs do the older fairies need to do for Summer?"

"Well, all the fairies have a job. They kind of grow in to it, I suppose, because you learn stuff then find your hum along the way. Like Beryn, she can do lots of different things, but her real job is making rain and frost and mist and stuff by helping the wind carry water. And have you met Uncle Mort? By the time you're his age you know pretty much everything there is to know! We do all sorts of things, like farewelling trees or creating snowflake patterns or putting the sweetness in strawberries. There's even a fairy who collects moonbeams! Hey, why are you sitting out here, Lelice? I thought you'd be in the forest getting to know the rest of us!"

Alice had been listening to Neiolith and had forgotten, for a moment, about Ngā Patupaiarehe and how she was going to meet them. She told Neiolith about her morning, about hearing Beryn's story and listening to Uncle Mort talk about the fairies in The Burrows.

"Oh, Ngā Patupaiarehe are so beautiful, Lelice! Their skin is like milk thistle and their hair grows so long and beautiful, the colour of sunsets. Oh, they are a lovely bunch of fairies! And their music – so gorgeous!"

"So you've met them?!" Alice asked eagerly.

"Oh, no, Lelice, I've never met them. Of course I haven't met them!" Neiolith rolled her beautiful gold-hazel eyes at such a ridiculous suggestion.

"Well, how do you know what they look like? How do you know they are beautiful?"

"How could they not be? Uncle Mort has told me all about them. I've heard their music once, and it made my heart burst!" Neiloth did a mid-air twirl for effect. "Only something truly beautiful could make music that lovely," Neiolith added. "And trust me, Lelice. I know beautiful."

8

Neiolith's Story

Once upon a time (oh, I've always wanted to say that!), a little flower opened up and inside was me! All around me, my brothers and sisters were emerging from flowers that looked like mine – flowers that had yellow petals, shiny with dew, and bright green stems. The petals were pulled up and out by the sun. Because they had been closed so long – all Winter, poor things! – the flowers were keen to stretch.

Mother and Father flew around us, welcoming us to the world. Fairies are born able to walk, able to fly, and if the hum is right, we can sing, too. I'll never forget the first song I heard; the soft, low beat that pulsed through the stem of my birth-flower. It got louder as my petals opened and then I heard my mother's voice singing with that earth beat. It was glorious! Mother and Father sang as the sun

52

drew us out of our birth-flowers and into the world.

And then, there was great sadness. Mother and Father stood together, their arms entwined, as they looked down on a flower that had not been enticed by the sun. The petals were dull and looked weighed down with the morning dew. The stem was green, but thin. It was a fragile wisp of a flower. I saw the grief of my mother and father and felt pain. This poor flower.

I flew over to this wispy flower on my wings, newly unfolded. I was so happy to have such beautiful wings, and yet my first flight was heavy. I was drawn to that little flower but I don't know why; maybe I felt that I should be with Mother and Father as they wept. My brothers and sisters were sad, too, but they were frozen in their sadness.

When I reached the flower, I touched it. The petals were cold. That just wouldn't do, so I *hugged it close, right under my chin. I held it for a while, Mother and Father watching me with love but great sadness. Oh, it was awful! But then, what do you know? I felt a little beat. It was a faint half-hum, moving up that skinny stem from the ground. All was not lost!*

And so, with a whispering voice, I begged the flower to open. I held the bud of petals in my hands and sang to it, softly, softly, with the half-hum that was climbing up the stem. Everything was quiet. Mother and Father watched on and my kin held their breaths. I wiped away the dew, pointed the flower to the sun, wondered what I was doing, and sang.

The petals opened slowly, slowly, the pale yellow tips peeling away at the top, one by one. But the hum was getting stronger, louder, so loud that my new family could even hear it themselves! But this was my song, and all they could do was listen and wait. Together we watched those petals unfold and reveal Greeve,

54

my most beautiful baby brother, pink-cheeked and sleeping soundly. He took my breath away with his beauty.

His flower, too, was not like ours. Pale yellow and stem-thin on the outside, yes, but inside, oh how beautiful it was! First of all, once it had unfolded, it was much bigger than ours – so big that it made the thin stem bend under the weight. And around Greeve was a pillow of deep, deep blue, dark like that midnight sky and soft like thistle seed. And the petals started crisp-apple red, then became pink, then orange, then yellow right at the tips. And on each petal, right in the middle, there was a bright purple spot encircled with a white line, a white so bright it shone.

When sweet Greeve woke to see his whole family, teary-eyed and open-mouthed, staring at him and his magnificent flower, he smiled and cooed and dazzled us with his dark blue, glistening eyes. Mother scooped him up, we gathered together, and I experienced the beauty of my family.

And so while other fairies fall in to their vocations by accident or work hard to be a part of something great, it seems I was, quite honestly, born in to mine. The song of beautiful things, of beautiful fairies, and of this beautiful world, is just too loud for me to ignore! I invite things that grow from the ground, especialy the shy things, to open up and share their dazzling beauty with the world. Because we all know, don't we? That real beauty is inside.

9

"Daddy." Alice had her best big-girl voice on.

"Allie." Her father had his best serious-but-trying-not-to-laugh face on. It made Alice even more determined.

"Daddy. Take me to The Burr – to the trees on the other side of the driveway. Please." Alice stared her father in the eyes. It meant she had to climb up on to the tall stool and kneel on a cushion to look at him across the sink as he did the dishes, but this was important. The dishwashing liquid was in her way so she moved it purposefully to the left. She didn't want anything between them, so he could sense the seriousness of the situation. She clasped her hands in front of her and waited for his response.

"No."

"Whyyy?!" She flopped down on the

bench and looked up her father with pleading, desperate eyes, big-girl voice all but gone.

"It's dangerous up there, Allie. Even I'd have trouble walking around up there. It's too steep."

"But I have to get to those trees!"

"Why? You've got all those trees on this side of the driveway, isn't that enough?" Her father was smiling kindly at her. Alice decided to cut him a break and come clean. She sighed.

"OK, Daddy. You can't have known this, but there are fairies up there, too." Her father lifted an eyebrow.

"I know!" Alice exclaimed. She knew he'd understand. "But they're different to the fairies that I know, they're called Patupaiarehe and they are afraid of humans. But they really don't need to be afraid of me. Do they, Daddy?"

"No, they don't, but I still don't want to take you up in to those trees, Allie. It's just too dangerous."

Alice huffed. She sat silently on the stool for a moment, watching her father scrub a plate.

"Daddy, how about the slip? Could you help me climb the slip, just a little way up? I promise I'll be careful and only go as high as you think we can." Alice waited, holding her breath.

"OK, Allie. Next weekend we'll climb the slip. We can probably go up about halfway. Your fairies will have to meet you there."

Alice was so happy she nearly fell off her chair! In a week she would have her chance to prove herself to Ngā Patupaiarehe, to show them there was nothing to be afraid of. More fairy friends! Alice couldn't wait.

10

It had been the slowest week Alice could remember, even slower than the week before Christmas. But finally it was Saturday morning! Alice knew it was early when she woke up, but she was just so excited, she couldn't stay in bed. She snuck not-so-quietly in to her parents' room and then, counting to three, leapt on her father. OOF! Her father woke with a fright and a frown until, of course, Alice spoke.

"Daddy! Good morning! Shall I make you some toast? With peanut butter and Mummy's apricot jam? I've put the jug on already, can you hear it? It's nearly boiling!" Alice was kneeling on the edge of the big bed, bouncing up and down. Her father was smiling now, even though he was rubbing his eyes. Alice knew that her father understood why she was so excited;

she'd only talked to him about going up the slip every evening this week!

Each day Alice came home from school, grabbed a banana or an apple or a craker, and ate it on the way to Kawakawa. Each day she'd linger on the driveway, gazing up at The Burrows, before heading to the forest or sitting on the tree stump to draw or play the ukulele or chat to her new friends. Each day, as Alice spent the afternoon talking to them or playing games, she learnt something new about the fairies.

The fairies had shown Alice how they make their beautiful soft clothes made from – as it happened – woven strands of thistledown. They taught her a new song, and she met Greeve, Neiolith's sweet little brother. In fact, she met lots of the fairies. They all knew her of course; but for Alice, it was like meeting long lost family. And each day she told the fairies her plan for

Saturday, when Daddy would take her up the slip and she would meet Ngā Patupaiarehe. By the end of the week she really knew that Ngā Patupaiarehe were shy fairies, because whenever Alice told her friends about her plans, they would just smile and shrug and talk about something else. She just knew that Saturday would be a very special moment, when she showed those Patupaiarehe that they didn't have to be scared of her.

And now, Saturday was here! Alice used up every ounce of patience while she waited for her father to eat breakfast. It was the first time in her whole life she'd finished eating before anyone else! It seemed to take forever but eventually, her father was ready to take Alice up the slip. They put on their boots, picked up a spade each, and made their way toward the trees.

Alice skipped ahead of her father,

swinging her Alice-sized spade alongside her as she went. She reached the edge of Kawakawa and stopped. To her father it would have looked like she was waiting for him, but actually she was seeing if any fairies were there. After all, they knew how excited she was too! At first she didn't see anything but after a few moments of focus, Alice saw the shimmer of fairies flitting in the trees. And then, there was Beryn and Neiolith. Alice grinned.

"Ata mārie, wee Alice. Off to the shops are we?" Beryn teased. Alice giggled and rolled her eyes, but Neiolith was mortified!

"Beryn! Lelice has been talking about going up the slip with Daddy for days and days! How could you forget?" Beryn blinked, and Neiolith went on, turning to Alice. "Well, *I* didn't forget, Lelice. Would you like some company up there? I'd love to come and see those beautiful fairies with you!"

Beryn looked suspicious. "That has nothing to do with Daddy going up the slip too, does it, young Neiolith?" Neiolith gasped with indignation but promptly closed her mouth in a pout, folding her tiny arms defiantly. Alice laughed, but noticed that her father was getting very close. Was he looking at her a little strangely?

"Yes, Neiolith, do come. That'd be great. But I might not be able to talk much."

Neiolith clapped her hands excitedly. "I'll meet you up there!" she exclaimed, and darted off up through the trees.

As Alice began to follow, Beryn laid one tiny hand on her arm. "Wee Alice. It's lovely you want to be friends with Ngā Patupaiarehe, but I really don't think you're going to see them today. I'm sorry."

Alice's spirits dropped a notch. "Why,

Beryn? Why am I so scary?"

Beryn fluttered closer. "Oh, you're not. It's just that they like to keep themselves to themselves. Just try not to be disappointed if they don't show. Promise?" She looked at Alice with clear, sparkling eyes. Alice could see that Beryn wasn't trying to be mean, she was just properly worried for her. Alice smiled her most reassuring smile. "It'll be great, Beryn, and I promise."

*   *   *

After a slippery climb to a ledge about halfway up the slip, Alice sat on a clump of grass. Her pants were muddy and her hands were covered in dirt, having slipped and tripped more than a few times on the way up. Her father had dug a few steps out on the way up and told her to use them to get back down if she wanted, but she was not allowed, under any circumstance, to go any higher. He had gone further up, however, to check the drain that had been damaged when the hill came down. So now Alice was sitting on the ledge, in the dirt, chatting to Neiolith.

Rather, Neiolith did lots of talking and Alice tried to listen as best she could while watching the trees. She couldn't see anything, though. She heard about how different flowers open and about how fairies can sometimes carry the scent of flowers around on their skin for a lifetime and about how once Neiolith opened a shy flower and inside was a sweet green frog. But she saw nothing. Not a flutter, not a single thing that shone or sparkled – with the exception of Neiolith – not even a bird. Just trees, kawakawa for as far as she could see. The Burrows were still.

11

Alice didn't go back into the house with her father when he came back from the drain. She asked if she could sit for a while longer instead, promising to not go one inch higher than the little clump of grass on which she sat. She explained that Ngā Patupaiarehe hadn't come out yet, and she wanted to give them more of a chance. Her father thought for a moment or two before nodding, digging a nicer path for Alice as he went down so she wouldn't slip so much. He was a good daddy.

Neiolith had long gone. The little fairy couldn't stay in one place for longer than a few moments, unless, of course, there was something intensely fascinating going on. This was not one of those times. And so, for a long while, Alice sat by herself just gazing into the trees of The Burrows, trying her best to not feel disappointed. After all, she had promised Beryn. But eventually she realised the truth: the fairies were right. Ngā Patupaiarehe were not going to come out today.

Alice slowly, slowly made her way to the bottom of the slip on the path her father had dug. She plodded sadly down the driveway and made her way in to Kawakawa. Then she sat by herself on the fallen tree in the clearing. She was wondering what she could do to earn the trust of Ngā Patupairehe when she felt movement in the air next to her. Alice was expecting it to be Beryn, or maybe Neiolith had come back. Imagine her surprise to find a young boy fairy, dressed in green, sitting next to her patiently.

"Hello?" He asked her.

"Hello?" Alice asked back. "What's your name?"

"I'm Bawn? I don't think you've seen me yet?"

Alice shook her head. "No, I haven't, but it's lovely to meet you." Bawn gave her a sweet smile and held out his hand for Alice to shake. She offered her index finger, which he put his whole hand on and waggled his arm up and down. Alice smiled.

"Why are you sitting here, Alice?"

Alice gave a little sigh. "I went to see Ngā Patupaiarehe. They didn't come. I guess I'm disappointed."

"Did they say they would come?" Bawn inquired. Alice was taken aback a little.

"No, they didn't..."

"Maybe they had a prior engagement?" Bawn offeredhelpfully.Alice felt a little giggle bubble inside. Perhaps they did!

"I haven't seen them before, I was hoping to meet them today," she said.

"Hmm." Alice recognised the same tone that all the fairies had used when Alice said she'd wanted to meet Ngā Patupaiarehe. She also realised that this was the first thing Bawn had said that wasn't a question. She couldn't dwell on it long, though.

"What do you know about Ngā Patupaiarehe, Alice?"

"Only what Uncle Mort told me last week."

"Can you tell me?" Bawn asked. Alice eyed him suspiciously. Usually the fairies seemed uninterested in talking about Ngā Patupaiarehe, or they didn't know anything other than *they keep themselves to themselves.* Bawn was the first fairy to ask *Alice* what she knew. And he looked really interested, too, sitting next to her on the fallen log, watching her with the question still on his face. Alice smiled as she decided to jump on the opportunity to share what she knew.

"Well, I first found out about them when Beryn told me about how she came to live in the little forest, travelling over the ocean in a coconut. And then I met Uncle Mort, who seems to be the only fairy who has ever met Ngā Patupaiarehe face to face." Alice paused, "*You* haven't met them, have you?" Alice asked Bawn. Bawn shrugged and shook his head. Alice shrugged herself, then continued her story.

"So. Uncle Mort told me that Ngā Patupaiarehe have lived on this land for longer than anyone knew, maybe even longer. He said that they come in all different sizes, most tiny like you and Beryn and Uncle Mort, but some as tall as trees. Uncle Mort said they mostly have skin the colour of blonde wood and their hair is usually colour of a sunset. Uncle Mort and Beryn said they are the best singers and flute players. Uncle Mort said that he's met other Ngā Patupaiarehe, from bigger forests, who like to play tricks on people and get humans into trouble. But he said most Ngā Patupaiarehe, like the ones in The Burrows, are shy and keep themselves to themselves. They don't like light or fire or the smell of cooking food. Uncle Mort said that lots of Patupaiarehe have been lost because they're running out of places to live. He said they are magic, not fairy magic like you, Bawn, or like Uncle Mort, but a different kind of magic. *Mauri*, I think Uncle Mort called it, a kind of special power you get from being a part of the earth for so long. Well, that's what Uncle Mort said."

Alice took a breath, encouraged by Bawn's continuous nodding. "Oh, and

72

he said there was a leader, too. Umm. Mati...something?"

"Matua Mōrehu?" Bawn offered.

"Yes! That's it!" Alice bounced in her seat with a burst of excitement. "So you know about them then?"

Bawn nodded. "I know that Matua Mōrehu was the one who found The Burrows and led his whānau there. They sing so sweetly, Alice, have you heard them? No? That's OK. And they can speak any language, like caterpillar or dog or baby human or fairy or flower. Matua Mōrehu is meant to be the best, a real kaikōrero for them all. And because he can speak like that, he keeps everything together, you know?" Alice nodded, even though she didn't really know at all. But it sounded wonderful.

Bawn continued: "Matua Mōrehu has kept his whānau together for thousands of years. When the fairies settled here it was decided that Ngā Patupaiarehe would live on the steep bank of The Burrows, where humans are least likely to go, and the other fairies would live down here, where we can make friends with humans. Like you, yes? You see Alice, living in these trees gives all the fairies here the best of both worlds."

"How do you know so much about Ngā Patupaiarehe, Bawn, even though you haven't met them?" Alice wondered. Alice didn't think a fairy could know as much as Uncle Mort, but Bawn seemed to know everything!

"I haven't introduced myself very well, have I?" Bawn shook his head, a little disappointed with himself. "Well, where should I begin?"

12

Bawn's Story

Have you ever found yourself in a place so dark that your eyes go as wide as they can? It's like they're being greedy, trying to steal as much light as possible. Maybe the clouds are so thick the stars can't shine through, or maybe the moon is nowhere to be seen, or maybe you've been stuck somewhere and the light can't reach you.

A very long time ago, I was trapped. I hadn't found my hum yet but it didn't matter; I was a young fairy with a taste for adventure. I was exploring a cave on a beach when suddenly the whole world shook, the earth's beat raced with fright, and the entrance to the cave was blocked with fallen rocks. For the longest time I was trapped. I couldn't talk to anyone, and I couldn't escape. But do you know what I could do? I could see, even in the complete darkness of the cave. Do you want to know how?

When the moon was full and bright, it shone right on the entrance of the cave as it rose over the water. I learned that even though the gaps between the rocks were too small for me, they were big enough to let tiny streams of light into the cave! Do you know what happened the first time I saw those beams of light? I heard something I'd not heard before. More than heard it, I think, I felt it. I didn't hear the earth hum like other fairies do, but I heard the light. I put my hand in to a moonbeam and felt the hum buzz up my arm. The light pooled in my hand and then dripped on the floor, sitting there like a water droplet before being soaked up by the darkness. As the light dripped off my hand I started to hum along with it. And you'd never guess what happened. The light stopped dripping! It held together like clay, forming a cool, glistening ball right in my hand! Can you imagine how happy I was?

I had a bag with me, for special treasures I found on my adventures. I tipped the treasures out onto the cave floor and used the bag to catch even more moonbeams, humming along with the light as I did. Soon my bag was filled with light! Which was good, because the moon was rising higher, and soon there were no moonbeams left.

I don't know how many times I collected moonbeams that snuck their way in between the rocks. Ten? Twenty? I can't be sure. But every full moon brought me a bagful of beams that I used to light up my cave. Because of that light I was able to explore right down to the back of the cave, to a tunnel, to a river, to glow worms that look like underground stars. The light from the moon helped me find my way out and I learned more about the hum of the earth, even though it was the hum of light that taught me. I think Ngā Patupaiarehe call this mārama, a word that brings the brightness of the moon and know-

ledge together.

I had been gone from my family for so long, trapped inside that cave. But I found my way back and we were so happy to be together again! And even though I didn't have my hum when I left, I had it when I returned. I left because I was looking for my hum in all the wrong places. Isn't it amazing how we can learn so much in the most unlikely of places? Sometimes the world can be so dark, but all it takes is a little bit of light! Now my hum was in my treasure bag, and in every full moon. I started collecting more moonbeams for my family and friends to use so they could light their way, too. There is so much in this world we don't understand, so much we can't see. But this is where I've found my hum. In the unknown.

Part Two

13

It was raining. Everything was wet and soggy and Alice was not allowed to go to Kawakawa. Usually she didn't want to go in the rain anyway – it could get slippery and her shoes always got covered in mud. But today was different; there were fairies out there waiting for her, and she had promised she'd be back! She still had so much to learn, especially about Ngā Patupaiarehe. She was going to meet again with Bawn to talk about them more, and Neiolith was going to show her how to make an unbreakable daisy chain! Alice hoped that the fairies would understand.

She was sitting at the table in the kitchen, looking out the window at Kawakawa. It wasn't far away, just past the barn, on the other side of the goats' paddock.

Alice tried to see the fairies from the kitchen, squinting her eyes and willing them to work better. She sighed and rested her cheek on the table. Already she had done all the puzzles in the toy box, drawn two pictures, rearranged the books on her bookshelf to look like a rainbow and even built a huge castle using all the wooden blocks. The day was dragging. Draaaaagging!

Alice still had her head on the table when there was a knock at the door. Alice walked to the door, shoulders slumped and feet heavy, and peered through the window to see who it was. It was Mr Burton, the man from next door, scowling like always with his hands clenched in fists at his sides. Next to him was Crank, his snappy little pug dog that went with him everywhere. Alice didn't like that dog. He was always coming to her house by himself, worrying the chickens and chasing her dog, Molly.

Alice opened the door a little bit and said "hello?" politely. Mr Burton tried to smile, but that just made him look like he had a bad tummy ache.

"Is your dad home?" he asked her. He always sounded growly.

"Yes, I'll go and find him," Alice said. She left the door open but didn't ask him in, which she knew was a bit rude since it was raining. But Molly was already hiding from Crank, whimpering quietly under the couch. Alice gave her a little smile and went to find her father.

* * *

Alice watched Mr Burton and her father through the window. The two of them were standing under the shelter of the open shed. Crank had crawled through the goats' fence and was chasing them around the field in the rain, naughty dog. Her father had his arms crossed, which was never a good sign. Mr Burton was pointing towards the trees, not to Kawakawa where her friends lived, but to the other side of the driveway, to The Burrows, where Ngā Patupaiarehe lived. It looked like Mr Burton was doing a lot of talking, while Alice's father was doing a lot of not understanding. After a while, Mr Burton walked back up the driveway, finally yelling at Crank to leave the poor goats alone. Alice hoped with all her might that Crank didn't go in to the forest and find her friends. And Alice's father stood for a while longer in the doorway of the shed, looking a bit sad. Alice didn't like it.

"What did he want, Daddy?" Alice asked when her father came back inside.

"Nothing, Allie, we were talking about the drain on the hill."

Alice thought her father was a terrible liar.

A little later on, Alice's mother came home from town. Alice was in the lounge, organising a few toys for a tea party, while her mother and father unpacked the groceries in the kitchen.

"Bill came down today," her father said.

"What did he want?" Alice's mother didn't like him very much, Alice could tell.

"He's selling another piece of land."

"Oh?"

"Yeah. The little corner of trees by our driveway up to their first paddock, we're going to have to sort out that drain." Alice stopped making tea to listen. Surely it couldn't be true. Only half of The Burrows was part of Alice's home – there was a fence that ran through the middle. But she knew that Ngā Patupaiarehe didn't care about silly things like fences. All those trees were home for them. Her mind was racing as her mother and father continued their discussion.

"Who would buy that? It's just trees."

"The sale will go through if Bill clears the trees and levels space for a house."

Alice's mother paused, but when she spoke she sounded as angry as her father sounded sad. Alice stopped listening to what they were saying, their voices becoming melancholy music for her sinking heart. What would happen to Ngā Patupaiarehe? To Matua Mōrehu and his whānau? Alice felt her eyes burn. What would happen to all her friends?

Alice realised that she could no longer hear rain on the roof. She looked out the window. It had stopped raining, and she noticed that there was even a little sun poking through. She wiped her eyes with one hand and threw all her toys in to the toy box.

"Mum! I'm going to Kawakawa," Alice announced, with her hands on her hips. Her mother opened her mouth to stop her, Alice thought, and then she smiled and nodded. "Wear gumboots please, my love."

14

Alice ran as fast as she could down to Kawakawa. Her heart was beating like the wings of a trapped bird. She didn't stop running until she reached the clearing, jumping over clumps of grass on her way.

"Beryn!" Alice yelled. She was breathless not from the run, but from the shock of her father's news. Luckily, Beryn was there in a heartbeat. Alice put her hand out in front of her and Beryn landed lightly in her palm.

"Wee Alice, what's the matter? My dear girl, is it that nasty Crank? He's gone now, there's nothing to worry about!"

"But there is, Beryn!" A fat tear rolled down Alice's cheek. Beryn gasped and let her wings lift her in to the air. She took hold of Alice's little finger and led her to the fallen log. The log was only a little damp, having been protected from the rain by the leafy branches high above. Alice sat and folded her hands in her lap, so Beryn sat on her knee and put both her tiny hands on top of Alice's. Alice felt wonderfully comforted by her little friend.

"Tell me what the matter is, wee Alice." Beryn patted her hand gently.

"Where's Uncle Mort? I think I should tell him, too."

"I'm here, you funny thing." Alice heard Uncle Mort's soft, gravelly voice near her feet. She looked to find the old fairy under a leaf, letting droplets of rain fall into a sack that was nearly as big as the fairy himself. Alice hadn't even seen him. She looked around and saw that she was surrounded by fairies. Many she'd met before but there were quite a few new faces, all looking at her with concern and shared sadness. Alice hadn't seen them because she rushed in, her brain full of woeful thoughts. She wondered if that was what happened to adults – they had lots of important stuff to think about. Was that how they forgot to see the fairies?

"Tell us, why are you so sad on this beautiful wet day?" Uncle Mort put his sack, now brimming with water and sloshing at the sides, down on the forest floor. He wiped his hands on his tatty brown waistcoat and looked up at Alice, love on his face. Alice wiped her cheeks on the inside of her sleeve and took a breath.

"Uncle Mort, Mr Burton is going to cut down trees in The Burrows. Lots of trees. And make a big flat space and put a house on it and people will live there and Ngā Patupaiarehe won't like it and they'll leave and they'll be lost, like all the others!"

Alice's eyes welled again as she looked down desperately at Uncle Mort.

She heard murmuring among the fairies around her, and a few gasped from shock. Uncle Mort just frowned ever so slightly. Beryn had let go of Alice and put her hands on her hips. She was hovering in the air, her face filled with fury.

"Let them come!" Beryn demanded. "Let them come and try and snap one little twig! We'll show them!" Uncle Mort smiled a small smile and shook his grey head.

"Show them what, Beryn?" Alice asked, dismayed. "What can we do to help? You're so little! *I'm* so little," she added sadly. This time it was Uncle Mort who comforted her. He pulled a kerchief from his pocket. It was giant by any fairy's standards, as big as a matchbox! Uncle Mort used it to soak up a tear on Alice's cheek.

"Wee Alice. We don't bother ourselves about what is little. We only care about what is lovely."

"Uncle Mort, aren't you worried?" Alice was suprised by his calm reaction to her terrible news.

"Oh no, Alice, I'm not worried at all. I'm too old for that carry-on. I'm sure you will think of something."

"Me?!" Alice squeaked. "What do you expect me to do? I can't stop them! I'm not allowed to cross the road by myself – how do I protect a whole forest?"

Uncle Mort shrugged. "You're not exactly alone though, are you my dear?" Alice looked about. The forest clearing was positively aglow with twinkling, tiny people, sitting or standing or hovering all around her. And while some of them still looked a little nervous, most had adopted the strong, defiant expression that Beryn so readily carried. Uncle Mort was right. Alice was not at all alone, she was surrounded by fifty or more fairies who had known her since she was a baby. They were kind of like her mother's family: there were so many of them she couldn't remember all their names, but she knew they all loved her nonetheless, and of couse she loved them back.

Seeing the fairies' faces, beautiful and glimmering and ready for anything, gave Alice hope and courage. She looked down at Uncle Mort, who was grinning like a child who had thought up the most wonderful game. It made Alice smile, the old fairy's taste for adventure. Alice took a deep breath and gave Uncle Mort a little nod.

"Bawn?" Alice called. "Are you here?"

There was a little commotion to the left of the clearing, and Bawn appeared from behind a small group of very young fairies.

"How can I help, Alice?"

"I want to know everything you can possibly tell me about Ngā Patupaiarehe."

"Where shall we begin?"

15

For weeks Alice wriggled in her seat at school, itching to get home to sit in the forest. She told her friends at school about the forest, remembering what Beryn once told her about how precious things can only be protected if people know about them. Lunch times were spent telling other children about the fairies she'd met and the games they'd played. Alice drew them, too, and wrote about them in stories. But then the school day would end, she'd arrive home and breathe a sigh of relief to find that not a tree had been touched in The Burrows during her absence.

For a few weeks, Alice sat halfway up the slip on a small plank of wood she'd found in the woodpile. There she stayed until twilight, when her mother would call her home. As Spring blossomed in to

Summer, the days got longer and Alice could stay later. One early evening she was still there when her father came home. He pulled his van to a stop at the foot of the slip. Alice, who had been doing her homework on her knees, looked up as he paused.

"Allie, what are you doing?"

"Just homework. I'm nearly finished. Can I come home when I'm done?" Her pen hung over her homework book, having been interrupted mid-sentence.

"Um, sure." Her father paused, before saying, "Why don't you do your homework inside?"

Without missing a beat Alice replied, "I don't know how long I'll have The Burrows, so I want to be a part of it while I still have the chance. I want to make it a part of me."

Her father looked at her thoughtfully

for three whole seconds before smiling and driving away.

Two days later it was the weekend, and her father had a suprise for her. The plank of wood Alice sat on was gone, being replaced by a low, stout table made of wood and a little wooden stool. They were both set firmly, safely in the earth on the edge of the slip. Alice was wide-eyed and filled with happiness at the little desk surrounded by trees. She had a good daddy, and told him as much.

Weekends were the best, when she'd often spend two full days at the edge of The Burrows, drawing or playing games with her fairy friends. This was, after all, her plan to try and save those trees. She wanted to be there to protect them from anyone that might come and try to cut down a tree; but she knew that to really save The Burrows she needed the help of Ngā

Patupaiarehe. To do that, she needed them to trust her. And so, when she was not doing school work or drawing or playing with her fairy friends, she talked to Ngā Patupaiarehe. She told them of her plans to help them, she complimented them on their beautiful, wild home. And she waited for a response, even though it didn't come.

But now, it was the summer holidays. Alice had six weeks to sit on the edge of The Burrows, to celebrate Christmas and the New Year and warmer weather with her magical friends. The holidays brought a lot of happiness to Alice because she'd heard her father say that over Christmas, at least, the trees and Ngā Patupaiarehe were safe.

It was during this time that Alice met dozens more fairies from her magic forest. She met fairies who had all manner of work to do, from sweeping the last pockets of

Spring pollen out in to the breeze, to helping the now grown pukeko chicks find courage to venture further from their loving mothers.

One fairy, Ferghan, was particularly intruiging to Alice. Ferghan seemed to be a little bigger than many of the other fairies, with long, muscular legs and a strong, solid body. She had long hair like the others but instead of wearing it loose, it was braided in two chocolate-brown ropes down her back. Instead of the soft flowing dresses of the other fairies, Ferghan wore pants of pale green and a top that looked almost black. She was not the same kind of diminuitive, petite fairy as Neiolith or Beryn, but she was just as fast, just as graceful.

The most incredible thing about Ferghan were her wings. Other fairies' wings were visible all the time, lying flat and open like a butterfly when they weren't in use. But Ferghan's wings, when she wasn't flying, were almost invisible. They folded against her back, narrow and slender, looking a little like an archer's quiver. But when she flew her wings were enormous, spreading out past her fingertips. They were dark blue mottled with glittering silver streaks. They looked like bird wings, not fairy wings, and although they shimmered delicately when she flew, Alice knew they were very, very powerful.

Ferghan was also one of the very few fairies who didn't come to Alice and spend a long while chatting or playing. She seemed very busy much of the time, and only managed a fast, full-face grin and a quick "hullo hullo!" when she saw Alice nearby.

One sunny afternoon Alice was

playing with little Greeve and Neiolith when Ferghan landed lightly on the tree stump across the driveway. Alice watched as Ferghan walked around the edge of the tree stump, jumping over the deep splits in the wood. Suddenly she crouched down low, her ear a mouse's whisker from the dark, rotting wood. Slowly Ferghan smiled and nodded.

"What's Ferghan doing?" Alice asked Neiolith.

"Hmm. I don't know, Lelice. She might be sending that tree further on its way. Then again, she might be inviting it back! Why not ask her? I've got to take Greeve home for a nap." The cherub-like babe yawned on cue. Alice stood and called down to the busy fairy.

"Ferghan? Hi! Do you have enough time to chat? I'd love to know more about you."

Ferghan straightened and smiled at Alice, wiping her forearm across her brow.

"Well, hullo hullo, pet! Sure thing, come down come down! I've got second or two!"

Alice walked carefully down the edge of the slip and across the driveway. She would usually sit on the tree stump here, but Ferghan was clearly doing something with it. She asked what was happening, and Ferghan winked.

"Look at the tree, Alice. What do you see?"

"I see a stump..." Ferghan gave a hearty chuckle, shaking her head.

"No no! What do you *see*? Really look!"

"OK, I suppose I see dead wood? There's lots of cracks, and bits are falling off."

Ferghan nodded proudly. "I did that."

Alice looked confused. "But Daddy chopped down the tree? It broke with the slip, it was dangerous."

"Yes yes, but I did *this*." Ferghan gestured grandly to the rotting lump of log before commanding, "Look at the tree again. What do you see on it?"

"Well, there's moss, and kind of puffy mushooms just there, and a little branch with leaves growing again. Oh, and look, a slater."

"Yes yes! I did all that, too!" Ferghan looked pleased as punch. Alice was humbled by her own befuddlement.

"Now Alice, look in there." Ferghan pointed to a particularly large split down one side. Alice leaned in.

"Oh my," Alice breathed. "What is that?"

"That, my pet, is an invitation."

16

Ferghan's story

Well well, where do I start? I suppose I start with the beginning. Let's go right back, to the day I was born.

Oh, how loud it all was! There were giants – GIANTS! Huge people moving about bits of stone to make buildings and roads and other such things, splitting stones and joining stones and just changing the way the world looked so it was easier for them. What they didn't know was that every little thing that those giants didn't make themselves, you know, the stuff that seems to happen by itself in its own good time, has energy. It has a special kind of life that helps it become. Yes yes, even a rock! And when that rock is broken, the energy has to go somewhere, it has to be something!

When one rock was split apart by a giant's hammer, the energy sparked in to life and I appeared. That's right, that's right, I was created by a stone and a giant clashing and crashing against each other!

As I grew, I learned a lot of new things. I learned that those giants were humans, of course, and I learned about sunsets, and the ocean, and about the different animals I saw. But mostly, I learned about things that grew from the ground. All around me I could see their energy, how life comes from one thing and grows in to another and then, as the leafy green things grow old, I could see that life leave it, back into the earth. Yes, the hum, the hum!

And as I watched the hum flow in to and out of all manner of plants and shruberies, I noticed something. I noticed how all that life that flows in and out of all things is shared. And eventually, when these living, growing things have become as often as they need to, they lay down to rest in the earth, and surround themselves in the hum for the last time.

But sometimes, the energy is not ready to leave. Sometimes, because of storms or greedy animals or those humans who were finding their feet, the energy was forced to leave sooner than the plant was ready. Oh, don't fret don't fret, it's not always a sad bad thing. Goodness, where would I be if that life wasn't pushed from the stone that I came from so suddenly? But it does create a little problem: what happens to the plant? Where does the extra energy go?

Yes yes, I found my hum.

I collect up the hum that escapes too soon. I reassure trees and flowers that might be a bit nervous about the big changes ahead. I help all things green and leafy to understand that, even if their hum goes and they have go back to the ground, there is plenty of energy to go around, they just have to be patient. And my most favourite part, I give little drops of life to plants and flowers who have rested, inviting them back to grow, to become again. It's a sad sad job sometimes, saying goodbye to such beautiful beings. But oh, how lovely it is, welcoming them back! I'm never perfectly sure if the invitation will be accepted or not. But trust, trust is the key!

17

It had been a beautiful, sunny summer, hot enough to eat ice blocks almost every day. And with not a single tree falling in The Burrows, Alice couldn't have asked for more! But now it was two days before school started back and the air was much cooler, with high, thick clouds turning the sky quite grey. Alice wondered if it was finally going to rain; the fairies loved the sun as much as she did, but the little stream was dry and their houses in the trees had become quite dusty. Alice crossed her fingers and hoped for a raindrop or two.

She was sorting out her pencil case, ready for school on Monday. During Summer she'd taken that case – and everything in it – all through Kawakawa, drawing pictures of flowers, of frogs, of ferns and of fairies. And now the case was filled with sand and a few broken pencils and precious stones and all sorts of other treasures – beautiful, but probably not so helpful in her classroom. She'd tipped out the contents on to her bed and was contemplating each object carefully before finding more appropriate homes for it all.

It was then that something unusual caught Alice's eye. At first glance it was little more than a twig, as long as Alice's finger and a very unspectacular brown. But there was something about this little twig that Alice found very familiar. She picked it up and squinted, studying the little stick. There was a twist at one end of the stick and little hole in the other. Goodness, it was Uncle Mort's stick! How did it end up in Alice's pencil case? She had to get it back to Uncle Mort quickly – she'd never seen him without it! Alice carefully pushed the remaining treasures in to a pile in the middle of her bed and raced out the door, Uncle Mort's stick held tightly in her closed fist.

Alice stopped running at the edge of the magic forest and took a deep breath. She remembered the day she'd gone in to the magic forest upset and hadn't seen her friends, even though they were all around her. Now she tried her best to go in to Kawakawa calm and slowly, because she saw much more that way.

As it happens, Alice had taken two steps in to the forest and saw Uncle Mort lying against a kawakawa sapling, enjoying the cooler breeze. Alice grinned.

"Uncle Mort, are you missing something?" She saw a sly grin crack Uncle Mort's old, lovely face in half.

"Never missing anything, wee Alice. Just without things temporarily, from time to time."

Alice tiptoed over to Uncle Mort carefully and sat beside him. She lay the stick beside him without saying anything. Uncle Mort glanced down.

"But they always find their way back," He said contentedly, resting his gnarled little hand on the twist in the wood.

At that moment, Alice heard a strange sound. Her curiosity became a deep, dark fear very quickly. Alice could hear humans. She looked around the tree canopy, trying to make her ears pick up every sound. Yes! There it was again! Human voices! Alice looked down at Uncle Mort, eyes wide with fright. Uncle Mort pulled his tatty little hat down to shield his eyes from the sun.

"Best go see what that's all about, wee Alice," he said sleepily. Alice was already on her feet.

She was up the slip in record time. The dry, hot summer had dried out the mud somewhat and it was much safer to climb. She stood by her outdoor desk and listened hard. Before long she heard them again: human voices, men's voices, talking to each other somewhere in The Burrows. She heard them tromping through the bush, making their way slowly down the steep bank. She heard her heartbeat in her ears, getting faster and louder as she listened to these men. Alice trained her eyes and focused on one particular part of the bush, where the trees weren't so close together and the fence could be seen. That is where the voices were coming from. They were getting louder. Alice took a breath.

"Who's there?" Alice called in her biggest, bravest voice. It sounded wobbly.

There was a few seconds of silence, and then, "Who's that?" a voice called back. Alice frowned.

"I asked you first!" Alice retorted,

indignant. Someone laughed and then, all of a sudden, there was a big, smiley man dressed in bright yellow clothing on the other side of the fence. He carried a big rope. Close behind him was another man, tall and happy looking like the first but only half as wide, dressed head to toe in orange. In his hands was a chainsaw. Alice's jaw dropped in horror.

"What are you doing here?!" Alice yelled urgently.

"We're just cutting down some trees. My name is Bear and that's Willy. What's your name?"

"I'm Alice," Alice replied, her eyes burning already with the threat of tears. She swallowed hard and squared her shoulders. "You're not allowed to cut down those trees, too many things live in them."

The men smiled wider and looked up at the trees. Alice watched them hopefully, but then the big one, Bear, smiled kindly at her and shrugged. "I'm sorry, but we gotta cut down these trees. You've got lots of trees over there that the birds and stuff can live in. Don'tcha? Look at it all. We won't cut down yours." He hooked the rope on the fence, turned to Willy and gave his arm a punch.

"C'mon, let's get the rest of the gear," he said, and they both disappeared in to the bush.

Alice was breathing heavily, wondering what to do. Her mind was working a hundred miles a minute, and she only had moments until the men came back. Her whole summer, as lovely as it was, came down to this moment. Alice turned to face the part of The Burrows on her side of the fence.

"Please, Patupaiarehe! Tēnā koa! Kei te haere mai a kōrero ki ahau! Please talk to me!" Through her pleading, Alice heard the men again, high in the trees. It sounded like one of them had lost his footing, and they were laughing about it. A tiny sob escaped Alice's throat.

She called again; "They're coming! Please come and show yourselves! They're going to CHOP down your HOME!!!" Alice was feeling well and truly frantic by now. She turned to see the two men at the fence again. Bear was looking at her strangely, while Willy was putting stuff that looked like ear wax on to a chainsaw bar. Alice breathed a silent groan of dispair and her eyes filled with hot, salty tears.

"Who are you talking to, Alicia?" Bear asked her.

Alice wiped her eyes and said, "It's Alice. And I'm talking to Ngā Patupaiarehe. Fairies." She sniffed.

Bear smiled at her, a sad, you're-a-funny-kid kind of smile. "Sorry, Alice." He looked up at the trees, humouring her.

"I don't see any fairies. They mustn't live in these trees."

Alice shook her head. "They live everywhere. Please, don't chop down their trees!" She added sadly, almost to herself, "I wish they'd just come out and show you."

Bear lifted a chainsaw and shook his head. He looked a little sad himself. "Aw, don't cry, bub. We're just doing a job. We aren't cutting down your trees, okay?" Alice just shook her head and turned back to her side of The Burrows. She called again, begging the mysterious fairies to come out, to show themselves and protect their own trees. But there was nothing, only silence, except for the men's talking somewhere behind her. Alice made her hands in to fists, she was nearly as angry as she was sad. Why wouldn't these Patupaiarehe come and help her! Just then, Bear called her.

"Hey Alice? We're gonna start the saws. They're loud, how 'bout you go home?"

"No, no, no, please don't do this," Alice begged. Her tears of frustration ran freely down her cheeks.

"Sorry, bub," Bear said, and he tugged the pull chord. The chainsaw spluttered in to life.

Heartbroken, Alice made her way down the slip as fast as she could and ran all the way home. As upset as she was, she didn't see Beryn and Neiolith hovering near by, watching on with their own sort of heartbreak as Alice pleaded with Ngā Patupaiarehe.

Neiolith watched Alice run down the slip, but Beryn kept her eyes on the men.

The noise was absolutely deafening, she couldn't even hear the earth hum with all that racket! She watched grimly as the bigger of the two approached a tree with the saw. He manoeuvred the clumsy piece of machinery into place, paused a second, and held the sharp, whirring blade against the trunk. A moment later the was a loud crack, a yell, and the man was on the ground!

Beryn flew closer to find the tree quite unharmed, the human pale and shaking, and the saw in hundreds of pieces on the ground. Beryn gasped and watched on with growing interest. While the bigger human of the two sat on the ground and looked decidedly ill, the smaller human picked up another chainsaw and pulled it in to noisy life. He went to another tree and, although confident in his intentions, he met the same fate. He ended up on his back, looking quite unwell. His machine fell to pieces after a mind-blowing explosion. And, most importantly, the tree had not one scratch.

With no gear and no nerve, the men quickly left the forest. Beryn didn't miss the look of bewildered suspision on the human's faces. She smiled to herself. Wee Alice had done it! She did a back flip in the air and turned to look at The Burrows, to see if she could see anything out of the ordinary. But there was just Uncle Mort, his staff in his right hand. He lifted his left hand in a wave. Beryn grinned. He'd heard Alice, too.

18

She knew her mother was worried. Alice had been so upset she couldn't talk, she just cried and cried until her eyes stung and there were simply no more tears left. Her mother had held her in a tight hug for a long while, taken her temperature, made her some warm milk, and asked her what was wrong lots of times. When her mother went to make lunch, Alice was tucked up on the couch with a huge soft blanket and a movie, even though the summer air was warm outside. But when Alice didn't even eat her most favourite lunch of ham sandwich and grapes, her mother turned off the television and looked at Alice.

"Little muffin, what's the matter? Tell me why you are so sad."

Alice took a big, deep breath.

"They have finally come to chop down

the trees in The Burrows, and I tried to stop them but they didn't listen to me. I'm just a kid. And Ngā Patupaiarehe won't even come and help!" Alice pounded her fists on couch in frustration. "So the tree chopper men sent me home because the chainsaws are so loud and now Ngā Patupaiarehe will have no where to live!" Alice started to cry again. "Why won't they just come out! They're such– they're so– they're just scaredy-cats!"

Her mother pulled her into another big, squishy hug and together they sat, a tangle of arms and love and blue fluffy blanket. However, after a while, her mother lifted Alice's head up and pushed her hair away from her damp, puffy face.

"Listen, my lovely. What can you hear?"

Alice listened hard. She could hear the fridge quietly whirring, and Molly's collar jingling as she scratched her ear. Alice closed her eyes and really *listened*. From outside came the noise of birds, of kihikihi, and there was a very faint rustle of leaves being blown in the gentle breeze. Alice felt very calm all of a sudden, listening to these quiet, soft things.

Then her mother whispered, "What can you *not* hear?"

Alice kept her eyes closed and really concentrated. She realised that she could *not* hear quite a few things. She couldn't hear a dog bark, or music, or her friends' wings beating the wind. She couldn't hear rain or a lawn mower or the zip on her pencil case opening and closing. Alice opened one eye and looked at her mother suspiciously. Her mother smiled.

"Alice, can you hear a chainsaw?"

Alice knew the answer straight away – she couldn't! In fact, she hadn't heard any chainsaw noise the whole time she'd been home. And she knew chainsaws; her father used them often to cut bigger logs that had fallen in Kawakawa. She knew they were loud enough to hear from the house. Surely they couldn't have finished cutting down the trees already?

Alice wiped her eyes on the back of her hand and said, "Mum, I think I need to go to The Burrows."

"I think you do, too. Be careful, dollface, and take your lunch with you."

*   *   *

Alice arrived at the stump on the driveway and was greeted by Beryn. She didn't say anything, just smiled a lovely, knowing smile, flew up close to Alice, and kissed her cheek. Beryn gestured to the slip, wordlessly inviting Alice to look at the damage done in The Burrows. Curious, Alice took a breath and and made her way up the slip. Her jaw dropped to find every single beautiful tree standing tall and strong, just as they had when she'd left them. She spun around to see Beryn hovering with Uncle Mort.

"They came?" Alice asked quietly, holding both hands out for the fairies to land in. Uncle Mort chose the hand holding the bunch of grapes, plucking one off for himself as he landed.

"That they did, wee Alice," he said, taking a bite out of the grape.

"They did?!" Alice was astounded and disappointed all at once. She'd waited weeks to meet them and now she'd missed them! "Why didn't they come when I was here?" she demanded.

"But they did, you called them!" Beryn said lightly.

"Did the men see them?" Alice exclaimed.

"Oh, no, they like to keep themselves to themselves."

Alice's brow furrowed. "But how did they stop the men? I don't understand."

Uncle Mort finished his mouthful of grape and lifted himself lightly off her hand.

"Come with me, wee Alice, I've got someone for you to meet. He can explain a little more about Ngā Patupaiarehe magic."

Alice followed Uncle Mort and Beryn down the slip and into the magic forest. The trio made their way through the clearings and up a steep hill to a little ledge. It was a part of Kawakawa Alice didn't come to often, but she loved it when she did. The air was cooler and it was a nice place to sit to take in the view. It was a peaceful, quiet place.

Uncle Mort lead her to a thin, old tree. The roots had pushed above the ground, making the tree base full of interesting nooks and crannys. And tucked in a nook, looking like a part of the tree himself, was a fairy. He was sitting cross-legged with his eyes closed. Alice stared, wide-eyed; this fairy made Uncle Mort look like a young fairy! This new fairy had gone quite bald, and his little face looked like one big wrinkle. His body was hunched over and withered like brown autumn leaves. He was completely still, so still in fact that a white cabbage butterfly had landed on his knee with not one hint of nervousness.

Beryn and Alice waited as Uncle Mort took off his hat and sat down next to the old fairy. For a long moment nobody moved; Alice held her breath, for some reason, as she watched these two ancient fairy men sit in silence, side by side. But then, ever so slowly, the two old fairies started to lean toward each other.

Uncle Mort had a lovely, soft smile tugging the corner of his lips, and his friend still looked like he was asleep. But eventually, both old fairies had leaned over far enough that their shoulders and temples were touching. And there they stayed, resting on each other.

After a while the old fairy opened his eyes slowly, gave the cabbage butterfly a little pat, and said in a gravelly voice, "Uncle, so good to see you, e hoa."

Uncle Mort sat up straight again and said, 'I've brought Alice. She has some questions for you, understandably."

Uncle Mort turned to Alice and Beryn and waved them closer. Alice tiptoed over the brambles and sat a little lower on the slope so she was almost eye level with the old fairy.

"Tēnā koe, Alice," the old fairy said. "Ko Akoni tōku ingoa." His voice was low and quiet and sandpapery.

Alice swallowed.

"Ko Alice ahau, Akoni. Kia ora."

Akoni smiled and he suddenly looked centuries younger. He may look crumpled like a leaf but he was young at heart, just like Uncle Mort. Alice could tell. She smiled back.

"Uncle Mort says you have some questions. I might be able to help you."

Alice nodded. "I suppose I want to know about Ngā Patupaiarehe."

Akoni glanced at Uncle Mort, who just smiled and shrugged.

"What do you need to know, Alice?" Akoni asked her.

"I want to know why they won't come and talk to me, even though I've said over and over that I won't hurt them and I'm sure they've heard me. And I want to know how they stopped the men from chopping down the trees. Do you know? Have you met them?"

Akoni nodded. "I've known them most of my long, lovely life, Alice. They're whānau. Are you comfortable there? Whakarongo ki taku kōrero, and I'll explain how they saved the trees."

19

Akoni's Story

I came here over the waters so long ago, I can't remember if it was night or day when I first felt it. I was in my home at the bottom of a volcano, huge and hot. My hum was strong then, and I was powerful. But then a great separation tore through the world. This land was created, and it called so loudly I couldn't ignore it. So I came. I haere mai au ki Aotearoa.

And here I found a new family, Ngā Patupaiarehe, fairies of fair skin and flaming hair and souls like the fires I'd left behind in my volcano. They were tricky and devious and always up to mischief. But they were loyal, loving whānau, protective and fierce. I loved them instantly. The hum that called so strongly led me to them. In all the mayhem of new trees and magic and life, I found them.

They are capable of so many things, Ngā

Patupaiarehe. Born of whenua wairua, they know this place better than anyone could ever dream of. They emerged in the great separation of land and sea and sky, and since that moment have lived a life of protection and celebration. And because they share their power with the land, as the land shares all of herself with them, Ngā Patupaiarehe can strengthen the lives of the trees around them. All they need do is push their wairua in to the ground, into a tree, into anything that's living, and the reciever is stronger than one thousand humans. A chainsaw is no match.

However, there is one thing that Ngā Patupaiarehe don't have. They have no language of their own. They can reach each other through the hum, of course, but they have no way of talking like you or me. That is until they hear someone or something speak. You see, Ngā Patupaiarehe are perfect impersonators. If they hear a dog bark, an owl call, a tiny tree frog croak, Ngā Patupaiarehe can make that language theirs. They use this skill to form friendships with the other living things in their forests and to confuse intruders. It's a clever but dangerous game they play, those Patupaiarehe. People can get lost, following the bark of a dog or the call of a lost child, but really it's a tricky Patupaiarehe up to no good, making mischief or protecting their home from humans who don't understand how precious it all is.

As time went on, Ngā Patupaiarehe were having to protect their homes more often. Animals that didn't belong here came with humans who spent their lives exploring new lands. And while some Patupaiarehe were happy to trick and decieve those humans who didn't understand, many Patupaiarehe just wanted to keep away from them, hidden in the shadows of dark forests and misty mountains, protecting these places as best they could. They were the ones that needed the loudest voice, a voice that could talk to the fairies who were starting to arrive in this place and ask them for help.

This is how I, Akoni, found the purpose for my strong hum, loud and powerful for so many years. I called the manuhiri, the visitors, to gather together, to help them in their role as kaitiaki and protect this new land.

I greeted the new arrivals, the fairies who were drawn to the hum of this land just like I was. I learned new languages, of fairies and humans, and taught all this to Ngā Patupaiarehe. While only a few faries have seen a Patupaiarehe, we all know about them, we all love them, we all respect their power. After all, they were here first. They share their home with us. They are the ones who hum the loudest, and yet, they depend on us all for help. Manaakitanga, e hoa, we will lift their power with our own.

Part Three

20

Alice felt her wet hair still dripping down the back of her T-shirt. It had been a long day at school, with the hot summer sun streaming in through the windows and making her sleepy. Thankfully, Alice's class were allowed to spend the afternoon playing in the pool while her lovely teacher read to them, her face hidden under her enormous fuchsia straw hat and blue-rimmed sunglasses. The swim completely revitalised Alice, so much so that, when her mother picked her up from school and asked what she'd learned that day, Alice didn't stop talking for one moment of their journey.

That is, until, they were on their own driveway. Alice looked to the left as she always did, to see if any Patupaiarehe were there. She hadn't been back up the slip since meeting Akoni, since hearing the story of Patupaiarehe and what they were capable of. But of course Alice was still hopeful to catch a glimpse of them as she drove past each day. This particular day, however, Alice saw something she didn't expect.

There was a huge, gaping hole in the forest. There were four or five busy-looking men, in fluorescent clothing, and the forest floor was covered in broken branches and trampled leaves. Alice cried out with fright, a noise that made her mother turn her head and see the hole in the forest, too.

"Oh, Alice, I'm so sorry, my darling."

"Please Mum please stop the car please!" Alice was so shocked she'd forgotten how to speak properly! She saw her mother hesitate, even as she brought the car to a slow stop just past the slip.

Alice was already undoing her seat belt.
She heard her mother call caution behind her as she flung the door open and ran back up the driveway.

Alice arrived at the site and was utterly heartbroken by what lay before her. She counted no less than seventeen tree stumps, their roots still strong in the ground but their bark in shreds and the trunks unnaturally smooth and flat on the top. Like a scar that ran right through the middle of cleared forest was the fence that separated Alice's home from Mr Burton's. It was lying on its side, twisted and slack. The men had cut down trees not only from Mr Burton's farm, but on her own. They had cut down her trees. Alice felt her eyes prickle as they filled with hot tears, not with sadness, but with anger.

"Hey!" A man's voice called out. Alice turned a little to see who it was, and recognised him instantly. It was Bear, the big, happy man who had tried to cut the trees a few weeks before. He still had a big smile that cracked his face in half.

"You can't be here, bub, you'll get hurt! You go on home now!" Alice was about to state her case when she heard something wonderful behind her.

"What on earth have you done?" Alice's mother had climbed the slip herself, seen what the men had done to the trees, to her trees, and looked as heartbroken as Alice felt. Bear's smile shrunk ever so slightly.

"Lady, you can't be here, it's dangerous."

"Evidently this is exactly where I am required to be." Alice's mother liked to use big words when she was upset.

"But we're chopping down trees!"

"Not any more you're not!" Alice's

mother put a hand on Alice's head and stroked her damp hair. Alice looked up at her and smiled, suddenly feeling very brave.

She turned to Bear and said, "You are not cutting down any more trees. We aren't moving, these are important and I won't let you cut down any more." Alice's mother added, "If we can't protect our own trees, our land, which you've trespassed on, who will?"

Poor Bear. He looked very confused and a little exasperated. He dropped the rope and big, heavy sack he'd been carrying and threw his hands in the air.

"Fine!" he huffed. "I'll get Mr Burton and you can have it out with him!" With that, Bear stomped off through the forest, back up the steep hill.

Alice gave her mother a tight hug, trying to squeeze as much love and appreciation into her as she could. Then together, holding hands, they carefully made their way through the maze of tree stumps. They got to the middle of the sad little clearing, to the spot where the fence would be if it hadn't been broken by the tree-chopping men. Alice's mother bent down, put a hand on a tree stump and said, "Ngā mihi mahana ki a Papatūānuku, i takoto nei," before sitting on the stump and pulling Alice on to her lap. There they sat, in a sea of stumps, waiting for the men to come back.

"Sweetpea, tell me about your friends again. Or maybe about Ngā Patupaiarehe?" And Alice talked.

21

Alice was starting to get a bit cold. Even though she sat on her mother's warm, squishy lap, her hair was still damp from swimming and the summer sun had dropped behind the trees. They had been sitting, waiting, for quite a long time. So long had they been waiting, in fact, that Alice's mother suggested that they go home and get warmer clothes.

Just then, they heard something in the distance. A branch cracking, a shout, the *thud, thud, stumble, thud* of someone walking through the trees. Alice and her mother were straining so hard to hear the muffled noise coming from their left that the noise of an engine on their right gave them quite a fright. Coming down the driveway at wreckless speed was a small, beat-up truck, its white paint smattered in dirt. Alice felt her mother take a deep breath; Mr Burton had arrived. They both stood up, planted their feet firmly in their forest, and waited just a little bit longer.

Mr Burton parked his truck at the bottom of the driveway and walked back up to the slip. Alice and her mother watched silently from their station as Mr Burton stumbled up the hill. He ignored Alice. Instead, Mr Burton said "hello" to Alice's mother, to which she replied, "How, exactly, do you intend to rectify this terrible, terrible mistake you have made?" Alice smiled and turned her eyes back to the forest to see the workers materialise in the trees.

Mr Burton replied, "Look, you have no say over what I do on my land."

"I'm not talking about your land, Bill, I'm talking about this!" Alice's mother waved her hand toward the patch of stumps. The workers were walking amongst them, making their way over to Alice and the adults. Alice's mother continued, "These are *our* trees. You've taken something incredibly important away from us. Away from Alice." Alice heard her name and looked up first to her mother, and then to Mr Burton. She could tell he didn't understand, even though he was apologising for it. Alice took a big, brave breath.

"Mr Burton. You have cut down the homes of lots of my friends. Well, my friend's friends, but they're important all the same."

Mr Burton looked down at Alice for the first time. She thought he looked bored. "There's just pests in these trees. You don't want them here, anyway. And look around, do you see any birds? They've already found other trees to live in."

"I'm not talking about the animals and birds, Mr Burton, although I'm sure they're not happy with you, either." Alice's mother snorted a suprised giggle. Alice looked behind her to see the workers waiting around, watching the conversation.

She turned back to Mr Burton and said, "I tried to tell them before, but they didn't listen and their chainsaws broke because of it. There are fairies in these trees and you can't – you absolutely cannot – cut them down."

Mr Burton's jaw dropped for a full two seconds, and Alice thought for a wonderful moment that he was shocked by the truth. But then he started laughing. A loud, mean, mocking laugh that invited the workers to laugh along, too. Alice looked desperately at her mother, whose face looked rather pink. Was she embarrassed by what Alice had said?

"I don't think you realise the seriousness of this situation, Bill," Alice's mother said. "You and all your men have trespassed. You've damaged property. You've cut down protected native trees. You have made an incredibly serious mistake and you're *laughing*?" She wasn't embarrassed, but angry. It gave Alice a little heart to know that she had her mother on her side.

Mr Burton wiped his eyes and said, "Oh, calm down. We'll fix your fence when we're done. And it's just trees, they would probably have to come down anyway. You can't expect anyone to build a house with bush on their back doorstep."

Alice's mother glared at Mr Burton, her lips tightly folded. Alice took a step back from her mother, for she was about to blow.

"It wasn't a mistake, was it?" Mr

Burton opened his mouth to speak, but Alice's mother rushed on. "You cut down our trees on purpose so you could sell the land! What, did you think we wouldn't notice?!" While Alice's mother got in to the swing of things, Alice saw her father's work van appear at the top of their driveway. She carefully made her way down the slip and met him on the driveway. She knew his heart would ache when he saw what had happened, and she wanted to be with him when he did.

Alice's father's eyes were already on the bare patch of forest, on her mother, and on the men.

"I'm sorry, Daddy." Alice apologised sincerely. "I couldn't stop them." Her father didn't say anything, but gave her a sad, loving look and a tight hug before taking her hand and making his way up the slip.

As the pair made their way back up

something caught Alice's eye. A sparkle, a flutter, and then suddenly, Neiolith and Beryn were hovering above the stump, waving frantically.

"Um, Daddy, I've just spotted something I've left at the stump. I'll be up soon." Her father nodded and kept walking up. Alice watched him approach the others and she heard Mr Burton exclaim over her mother's voice, "Ah, finally! Someone I can reason with!"

Alice didn't hear what her father said, for her mother's exasperation was just too loud.

Alice apologised again when she reached her friends, but they wouldn't have any of it.

"Oh, Lelice, don't be a silly sack! We're here to help!" Neiolith grinned. "My goodness, this is just so exciting! A real revolution! Come on Beryn, let's show 'em who's in charge!"

Alice smiled and looked at Beryn. "You're going to help? But how? They don't see you and they're not listening to me."

Beryn nodded. "It's true, wee Alice, they're not taking any notice." She flew close and Alice put out a flat hand so Beryn could land. The little fairy put her hands on her hips and smiled slyly. "We will just have to demand their attention, won't we?"

Alice looked up. It wasn't just Beryn and Neiolith anymore, but Bawn was there, too. And Ferghan, and even Akoni was there, fluttering as gracefully as the others. And dozens of other fairies, carrying bags and little lanterns and flowers and all sorts of other tiny, magical things. Beryn lifted herself in the air as Alice's chest swelled with hope.

"You're our voice, wee Alice, and the

voice of Ngā Patupaiarehe. They will hear you now."

22

Alice, Beryn, Neiolith and the others made their way up the slip. The adults were being awfully loud; Alice didn't think Ngā Patupaiarehe would like that at all. She looked around, but of course she couldn't see them. Someone else was missing, too. Where was Uncle Mort?

Alice reached her mother and held her hand. She put her other hand on her mother's arm; a signal that Alice was waiting to talk. Her mother finished her long, complicated argument before looking down at Alice. Alice, however, turned to Mr Burton. He was looking rather red now, and not at all pleased with the situation. Her fairy friends were hovering around behind him, bright and shimmering among the angry, unseeing adults.

"Mr Burton," Alice began, "Ngā

Patupaiarehe used to live in those trees. We can fix your mistake but you really can't cut down any more trees. I won't let you." Mr Burton looked at Alice's mother and father, who just shrugged. But Alice didn't see that, for she had turned to the trees that were still standing in The Burrows.

"Tēnā koutou, Ngā Patupaiarehe. I don't need to see you. I will stop them from cutting down any more trees, I promise." Alice heard Mr Burton tell her mother to take her home because she was just wasting time, but Alice kept talking.

"I'll protect you, you stay right where you are." Mr Burton moved behind her but Alice's father rasied his voice, stopping him in his tracks. It didn't stop Alice.

"Aroha mai, aroha atu, e hoa mā, and you being safe is enough." Alice called to the trees.

"For goodness sake," Mr Burton

shouted, "Fairies aren't REAL!"

Alice turned slowly to face Mr Burton.

"I don't care about what is real," Alice assured him, "I only care about what is lovely."

With that, the fairies gave a whoop of excitement and flew in to action.

While many of the fairies flitted off with their lanterns and satchels, Akoni and Beryn stayed nearby. Slowly but surely, Alice saw Beryn change. Her eyes closed, her skin brighter than usual, Beryn hovered in front of Alice and slowly started fading. Soon Alice could see *through* her! Worried, she looked at Akoni for reassurance. He nodded and gestured to the sky, and Alice was amazed by what she saw. Falling down softly over the trees was a think blanket of mist. Beryn, whose hum lay in the moisture in the air, was using that special power of hers to create a foggy roof over The

Burrows.

"Mum, look!" Alice pointed upwards, and together they watched the mist come down. Soon all the adults were looking; even Mr Burton glanced up and commented how strange it was, having fog in the middle of summer. Before long, a thick white haze had created a dome over The Burrows. She remembered that Ngā Patupaiarehe used to live in the mist at the top of mountains. Alice sighed with relief and gave Beryn, who looked like her old, lovely self, a knowing smile. She had hidden Ngā Patupaiarehe; they would be happier now.

Then, Alice felt something on her shoulder. It was Akoni. He had landed on Alice to get her attention. He stroked her cheek; his hand was very warm. Then with a wink, his wings lifted him in the air and suddenly, everything was still, as if taking a breath. Then, as the adults lost interest in the mist and went back to their argument, Akoni sang:

> Te ngahere, ngā rākau,
> Te wairere, ngā roimata.
> He taonga ēnei, ka mate, ka ora,
> Me aroha ā muri ake nei.

Akoni's gravelly voice rang out through The Burrows. Alice didn't know what he said, but the fairies did. The forest did, too, and Alice felt it exhale with contentment. Of all the adults, only Alice's father looked around for a moment.

Akoni sat on a stump at Alice's feet, looking tired. She offered him a hand to rest on and he happily climbed aboard. She thought he felt cold now, so she cupped her hands a little to warm him.

"Are you all right, Akoni?" Bawn was suddenly fluttering at Alice's side. Akoni nodded gratefully.

"Is it my time yet?" Bawn inquired. Akoni shook his head.

"Look, Bawn. Young Alice, look at what they're doing."

There was a hive of activity among the tree stumps; the area was positively glowing! Alice noticed Ferghan – her larger body and swiftness made her stand out like a beacon. She had a little satchel slung over her shoulder, the weight of it not at all affecting her strong, bird-like wings. She was darting like a fantail from tree stump to tree stump, spending a few moments at each one before moving on. She spent longer with some of the stumps, and occasionally she'd call Neiolith over to join her. They worked quickly, the concentration plain on their faces. Alice noticed that after Ferghan left a stump, another fairy would hover close by it and stay there. Soon, Ferghan had visited every single stump and the site was no longer a hive of activity, but a vigil.

"Now?" Bawn asked Akoni excitedly. The old fairy chuckled.

"Yes, young Bawn. Go and speak to them."

As Bawn flew off to the adults, much to Alice's suprise, Ferghan arrived at Alice's side. She looked flushed and shimmering and bursting with energy. Turning to the stumps, Ferghan called, "OK, OK, my beauties. Go to sleep now."

And chaos ensued.

23

Everything happened in a moment. Workers who were sitting on stumps suddenly found themselves on the ground. The air was filled with a damp, musty smell, like wet leaves in sunshine. Most of the adults had stopped talking in awe and fear, with only Mr Burton continuing his rant, completely oblivious to his surroundings. Alice's jaw dropped, then her face broke in to a giant grin. And the fairies glowed so much they looked like stars. Because, you see, in a single moment, every stump that had been cut so thoughtlessly had suddenly become small piles of rotting, damp, dark-brown bark, their energy floating like fireflies in to the waiting embrace of the fairies. The tree stumps had died, right before everyone's eyes.

Alice looked to the gaggle of adults and noticed something. Bawn, not shining yellow like the other fairies but glowing with a white-blue hue, was on her mother's shoulder. He was whispering in her ear and soon, Alice saw her mother's face change. It wasn't fearful any more, but soft and knowing. It matched her father's face; Bawn had already spoken to him. Bawn went to the workers as well, one by one, and Alice saw their faces change, too.

"Mum," Alice whispered, "Did you hear him?"

"Hear who, baby girl?"

Alice's heart sank for a moment, but soared in the next, as her mother said, "You see, Alice? Adults forget how to see and hear fairies. I'm so glad you still can. You keep listening to them, and tell us what they say."

Alice's father came over to them both.

"Allie, do your friends mind me taking the wood for our fire?"

"Oh, no, Daddy," Alice grinned. "My friends *love* you." Alice looked over to Neiolith and winked, the little fairy herself somersaulting in the air. Alice's father said something about the wood, but Alice didn't hear him. Something was happening in The Burrows.

Yes, she could hear it. Alice could hear music. It was so quiet, so soft, so delicate that it was being sucked out of her ears by Mr Burton's raging.

"Mr Burton, please!" Alice raised her voice, causing a break in Mr Burton's incessant noise. But that little break was enough; whatever was making that music took advantage of the silence.

The haunting notes of a flute-like instrument filled every space of the forest.

Everyone – even the adults – held

their breath as the beautiful music floated down from the mist and settled over the man-made clearing. Even the fairies were still, their faces tilted up to The Burrows. Only Bawn continued on his way, whispering in the ears of the workers. Alice felt her heart ache with the beauty of what she heard; she had goosebumps on her skin and her whole body filled with joy. In all her life she would never again hear something so beautiful, so real. Alice listened with all her might, for she did not want to forget the way this music made her feel.

"Oh, Alice, what kind of magic is this?" Alice's mother breathed. Alice, however, didn't have time to answer. Neiolith had shaken herself from her entrancement to sing along with the music, flying slowly around the clearing.

Neiolith's sweet voice was not as loud

as the flute music, it was tinkling like soft rain on a tin roof. But as she flew, and as she sang, Alice noticed that the fairies she passed were roused from their daze, and they placed the little drops of glowing energy in to the piles of dying bark. Soon, the energy was gone, and the clearing seemed quite dark.

When she was done, Neiolith came to hover next to Ferghan. They held hands and looked at Akoni, warmer now and flying near the top of the slip. He nodded and the two fairies grinned. Turning to the clearing, Ferghan and Neiolith, two fairies so different in appearance, blew a kiss towards the piles of dark wood.

The music stopped. The piles glowed with the light of a hundred moons. From the piles sprouted dozens of saplings, growing as tall as Alice within seconds.

And from high up, from the top of the

tallest tree in The Burrows, came the laugh of a child.

Alice grinned. Those tricksy Patupaiarehe! All the adults reacted with amazement, laughing or gasping or pointing with awe. All, that is, except Mr Burton. Bawn was on his way to Mr Burton; but the sprouting trees and laughing Patupaiarehe had given Mr Burton a monstrous fright. He took off like a bolting horse down the slip, slipping himself as he went, running away from the strange events of the magic forest before Bawn could share some wisdom with him. Bawn shrugged and joined the celebrating.

Before long, the mist disappeared and the clearing, now thick with saplings, was bathed with the final rays of mottled twilight sun. The workers apologised to Alice and her parents for cutting down their trees, and Bear gave Alice's mother a small card. "Call my brother, he'll fix this fence for free," he said. They went down the slip themselves and Alice was left with her parents, surrounded by her friends. They looked mighty pleased with themselves.

She held her father's hand as the trio made their way down the slip. Out of habit, she turned to gaze at The Burrows before leaving. There, right at the edge of the clearing, was Uncle Mort. He looked happy, if a little tired. He was holding his staff up, as if saluting her. Alice waved, happy to see him, but confused. Why hadn't he come to help? Uncle Mort smiled back, gave a little bow, and disappeared into the trees.

24

It had been a while since the men came to chop down the trees. Alice visited her fairy friends almost every day after school, doing her homework in the clearing and watching summer turn to autumn. Ferghan was as busy as ever, helping flowers get tucked in, ready for the colder months. Alice and her fairy friends watched the spring chicks take flight and leave the forest, while Greeve climbed in to the empty nests of lonely parent birds and offered himself for cuddles and love. The frog song that floated up from the dam was Alice's cue to get home each twilight. Many a late afternoon she sat with Akoni, scratching the ground with long sticks and feeding the friendly fantails, just as Uncle Mort had done when she first saw him. Alice's father was unsure of going in to Kawakawa at first, but Alice soon assured him and many weekends were spent in the forest with him, Neiolith swooning nearby. Twice Alice's mother released new friends in to Kawakawa – a hedgehog and a young keruru – and Alice watched them find their place amoung the living, breathing life within the kawakawa trees.

As summer slid into autumn Alice played, sang, sat, and learned in Kawakawa with her friends, and yet she didn't see Uncle Mort. None of the other fairies seemed to be worried about his absense, so Alice decided not to worry, either.

The saplings in The Burrows that had sprouted so suddenly from the ground were now as tall as Alice's father, with strong, straight trunks and leafy green branches. These trees were oblivious to the changing season, or they simply didn't care. The long, dry summer had sucked much of the moisture out of the ground and the slip leading up to The Burrows had become hard and cracked. It was the safest the slip had ever been, since Alice's father had allowed her to go up there by herself. And yet, Alice had only gone back to The Burrows once since the evening when the trees had been cut.

A few weeks after the men had been in The Burrows, Alice's class made things with clay. Her teacher said they had to give the first thing they made to someone special, a taonga that needed to be shared. Alice made a duck, and left it on the table on the slip. She said in a quiet voice, knowing that Ngā Patupaiarehe would hear her, that this taonga was for them and she was still looking out for them, even if she didn't come and visit. The duck sat there for a few days before disappearing.

Mr Burton left to live somewhere else

soon after his tremendous fright in the trees. He sold his house and left his sheep and moved in to town. Alice's father said he was living in an apartment high off the ground, with not a tree to be seen. Alice felt a bit sad for him, but she was glad that Crank wouldn't be running through Kawakawa any more. When she told the fairies, only Bawn didn't cheer with joy, but instead wondered aloud, "What would he be like if I managed to talk to him?"

Things were peaceful in Kawakawa. Alice had a whole group of fluttering fairies for her closest friends, friends that were safe and happy. Alice invited other friends to the forest, her cousins who delighted in the wildness of the trees and her friends from school who came to feed the goats. None of them could see the fairies but that didn't matter; they knew they were there, because Kawakawa was so obviously special and Alice had told them the stories.

It would be a long, long time before Alice would forget those stories. And even though her family didn't see the fairies, they knew they were there and they would find it hard to forget, too. The adventure was too big to forget! Every day in Kawakawa she saw more, knew more, felt more. And while Alice knew that the forest was becoming a part of who she was, she also knew that she was a part of the forest. She was its guardian, its protector. Akoni called her a kaitiaki; someone with enough voice and enough strength to take care of something else. It seemed that Alice had found her hum.

But right now, there was nothing to protect her forest from. All was right in Kawakawa, and in The Burrows. The fairies were real, and they were lovely. And they all lived happily ever after.

25

Uncle Mort's Story

I didn't really know about the hum until my good friend, Akoni, came to Aotearoa. We were happy enough on the back of Papatūānuku, and what Akoni called the hum was just our way of speaking to her. Akoni wasn't sure why the hum had called him at first, but until it was made clear, he spent time teaching us his language and learning our ways. It didn't take him long. Akoni had a force like fire and voice to match; soon he was one of us.

Other fairies were also drawn to our whenua ataahua by the hum. We like to keep ourselves to ourselves but we watched those new fairies from our homes deep in the forest, and we saw that they loved our earth mother like we did, so we allowed them to stay.

After many, many risings of Puanga, humans arrived. Some spoke as well as they could to Papa and her children, and they tried their best to work with Papa, not against her. My family had a wonderful time with them, playing tricks and learning the languages of their animals and children to draw them in to all sorts of tricky predicaments. But they left us taonga and played games with us too, and for the most part, we got along well enough.

But others came, on ships with wings, with animals and with fire they sometimes couldn't control. They were so loud they couldn't hear Papa, and it was clear they had long stopped trying to. Their arrival made our world a scary place. The smell of their cooking was awful and they were determined to light up every dark place, no matter what time of day or night. We hid ourselves at the top of mountains, but as they ventured wider, growing bigger and more fearsome, we needed a kaitiaki.

Akoni, my dear friend Akoni, called the new fairies on our behalf. The new fairies *weren't so concerned with the humans and so they sought out safe places for us to live. As it happens they brought us here, to The Burrows, where humans didn't stray. Close by was a home for Akoni and his new kin, a kawakawa grove where only the most gentle humans enjoyed the gifts of Papa. I decided I needed to thank those fairies who had found this safe little wrinkle on Papa's back. I had to hide who I really was, of course. My whānau were worried that if the new fairies knew of one Patupaiarehe, they'd want to know them all!*

Well, when I met that mismatched bunch of fairies that had found their home here, I was shocked. They were kind and loving and able to not only hear the hum that Akoni had felt all those years ago, but they, too, could use its power in wonderful ways. I fell in love with them all.

None of them know who I am, of course; they know that Patupaiarehe are reclusive creatures and would wonder why one was venturing from The Burrows! And so, in Kawakawa, I am Uncle Mort, an old man who disappears from time to time. I disappear so I can go back to being Matua Mōrehu, back to my whānau, back to tell them we are still safe. I suppose you could say I'm the tricksiest one of them all!

About the Author

Tiffany loves words. Although she's been writing all her life, this is her first book.

When not writing fairy tales, Tiffany is a teacher, a marriage celebrant, a student, and an enthusiastic collector of books.

Tiffany lives with her partner, their two daughters, and a collection of animals on a little farm near Whanganui, New Zealand. A surprising amount of *Fairies of Kawakawa* is true, and Tiffany loves the little forest on the farm almost as much as Alice.

Made in the USA
Coppell, TX
15 November 2019